BUILT TO LAST A LIFETIME

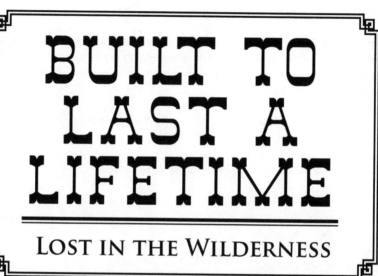

BUILT TO LAST A LIFETIME

LOST IN THE WILDERNESS

A novel of old Kentucky

Book One

DR. ERNEST MATUSCHKA

ELIZABETH DURBIN

iUniverse, Inc.
Bloomington

Built to Last a Lifetime
Lost in the Wilderness

iUniverse books may be ordered through booksellers or by contacting:

iUniverse
1663 Liberty Drive
Bloomington, IN 47403
www.iuniverse.com
1-800-Authors (1-800-288-4677)

ISBN: 978-1-4759-5375-6 (sc)
ISBN: 978-1-4759-5376-3 (ebk)

Printed in the United States of America

iUniverse rev. date: 10/05/2012

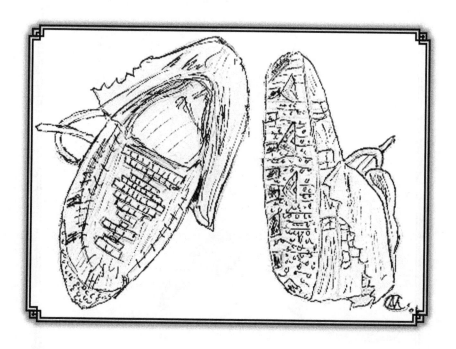

INTRODUCTION

To the Reader:

This is a novel of old Kentucky, set in the late 1700s or early 1800s, at about the same time that Daniel Boone was making his reputation. It was a time when people from the eastern states could move into the Kentucky territory and stake a claim on land, provided that they built a shelter, cleared some land, and raised a crop.

This is a historical novel, which means that the history and setting are accurate but the people are fictional. The dialect used in this book reflects the language style that was spoken by the early settlers in Kentucky.

It should be noted that while there is adventure in this book, there is a minimum of descriptive violence and an absence of sexual content. It is written for students from grades four through high school or for anyone who may enjoy a book of high interest and lower vocabulary levels.

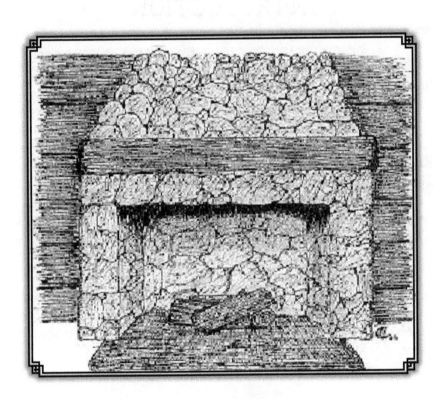

CHAPTER ONE

A Feeling in Her Bones

Sarah knew she should get up. It was still dark outside, but Gramma was up and stirring the fire. There was a full day's work for her. At age fourteen, Sarah was expected to work like a grown woman. As she lay in bed, she thought of her mother, Lizabeth. Her mother was her role model and someone that she admired. It pained Sarah to remember her mother, since she had died of a fever last fall. Sarah never felt so alone or vulnerable. She loved her mother, and no words could describe the loss she felt.

The burden of raising the family fell on Sarah and Gramma. Gramma was her mother's mother. She was of good German stock, having arrived in Pennsylvania from Germany. Grandpa Asa was also German and would correct anyone who called him Pennsylvania Dutch. He would say, "We ain't Dutch, we are German."

Hard work was expected of Sarah. She had taken over the raising of the two younger children, Ben and Mary. Ben was a three-year-old who was into exploring everything. He could be made to mind, but most of the time he was off looking for excitement. Mary was two, and his shadow, as they were constant companions.

"Sarah, Sarah."

"Yes, Pa."

"Sarah, it's time to get up," Pa whispered.

"Yes, Pa. I'll get right up." Sarah stepped out of bed onto the cold floor. She stretched and yawned. She was becoming a tall girl, like her mother. Lizabeth was tall and muscular. Sarah had Lizabeth's blond hair, except Sarah's hair was a deep gold. Both parents, as well as all the children, had deep blue eyes. Sarah slipped off her nightgown and, turning her back to the room, slipped on her dress. Her first job in the morning was to make the corn meal mush ready for breakfast. If there wasn't enough corn meal, Sarah would have to grind some.

"Is Nathan up?" asked Pa.

"I don't reckon," Sarah replied.

The household was still dark and getting ready for dawn. They didn't light candles in the morning. A waste, Gramma would say, as candles were in short supply. In fact, almost everything one used over the winter was becoming in short supply.

Gramma always busied herself getting the fire going. She rarely talked in the morning, which Sarah missed, as she and her mother had usually kept a running conversation going from dawn until dusk. When Sarah thought of her mother and a baby sister she really never got to know, she developed a sharp pain in her stomach.

Pa would get up and head out the door to take care of the outside chores. Sarah knew that he would visit the graves every morning, and she knew that he was still grieving. This was a sad family, trying to survive the winter and make it into spring. Only Nathan seemed to be in good spirits most of the time. He was all boy and loved to hunt and fish. He was too young to go off into the forest alone and hunt, but he could go down to the creek and fish when the ice melted. At almost thirteen, Nathan was developing into a fine young man.

Sarah appreciated Gramma's silence. She knew that as soon as Gramma started talking she would begin demanding work out of everyone. It wasn't long.

As she laid aside her mending, Gramma said, "Land sakes, Luke, seems like a body just can't keep up with all the work that's to be done just to keep body and soul together around here. Looks like it should be warm enough that the dandelions will be up under the leaves to make a mess o' greens. My old mouth is lookin' for the taste of fresh greens."

"I've been thinkin' on it, Gramma. If I take it easy, I can go over the ridge and see if I can scare up a deer. The young'uns are needin' meat. I should've gone earlier, but now the snow is gone, I can go without fearin' that my foot will be froze again. If it's a good sky tomorrow, I'll go early, probably right before sunup. I might have to go a long way to find one, so don't worry if I don't get back 'fore three or four days. If I get a good buck, it'll take me that long to pack it back." Luke leaned over a shot pouch he was mending and looked at Gramma.

"You be careful, Luke," she said. "I heard a screech-owl last night and the night before. That ain't a good sign. I don't know how the little ones and I could do without you. Do you want me to fix some food to take with you? Land knows, there ain't much, but I could find you a few pieces of jerky I saved back in case we had more bad weather."

"A couple of pieces of jerky would be fine. Tomorrow Nathan can go down to the stream and cut him a pole. I'll fix him a fishhook, and he can try to catch some fish for you. Now that the ice is broke, maybe he can get some. They would taste mighty good."

Luke limped over to the shelf on the wall and got down the mold to make lead balls for his rifle.

Gramma watched him anxiously. His foot still wasn't right from when he froze it in the blizzard, she thought. She wished Luke wouldn't go, but they needed meat. She couldn't explain the feelings that she had. Luke would think she was just a foolish old woman if she would tell him. Something was not right. But try as she might, she couldn't put down the feelings of dread.

*   *   *

Gramma was usually strong-hearted. She'd walked over the mountains with Luke and Lizabeth. She had kept her pace, carried her heavy load, and never regretted leaving the home place in Pennsylvania to come to this wilderness. But since the sickness that took Lizabeth and little Beth, she just couldn't take heart. Seemed like something in her went with them.

Well, she'd better put the starch back in her backbone, she thought. She'd have to take care of the young'uns until Luke got back. They'd all feel better when they'd got a bellyful of meat.

"I'm just worn out, tired, hungry and old. When you get old, you get fancies," she told herself as she rubbed her old, gnarled hands together.

Stiffly, she got up from the stool by the fire and went over to make sure that Ben and Mary were covered against the cold that would come when the fire died down. Her hand lingered over the quilt she had made from many different pieces of fabric left over from clothing that earlier she had made for her family. She cherished the quilt for its memories. She smoothed it with a calloused hand and remembered . . . that piece had come from the dress she wore when she married Asa; this one from a dress she had made for Lizabeth when she was three.

Lizabeth had said the quilt was too heavy to pack on her back over the mountains, and Gramma had almost agreed, but now she was glad she had carried it. It was a reminder of her husband, Asa. She remembered his tall, lean, muscular body even as he grew older. They were both hard working and were aware of each other's stubbornness. But Asa, with his long gray beard and twinkling blue eyes, had loved her deeply, and she felt his loss.

She had better go to bed. Tomorrow she would use the last of the fat to make soap. She had put it off too long, and they were running short. "They might be hungry, but they'd starve clean," she muttered to herself. She went outside for one last look at the stars. "It says in the Bible that the Lord watches over us. I've got Asa watchin', too. It won't be long 'til I'll be with him. I'll just have to wait a little while longer, 'til Nathan and Sarah and Ben and Mary are a little older." The two older children can almost take care of themselves, but Ben's a bundle of energy and Mary will need some extra care. It's unfair to Sarah to saddle a fourteen-year-old with being a mother to two babes, but the times dictate her life.

She checked once more to assure herself that two blond heads were poking out from under her quilt. "Good night, dear grandchildren," she whispered.

Gramma went to the bed she shared with Sarah. Nathan was asleep in the loft. Soon, Luke would join him. Peace was settling into the cabin.

The fire flickered as Luke took the melted lead and carefully poured it into the mold. Gramma didn't like the way the flames flared up. Another sign? "Old foolishness!" she sniffed, and rolled over, courting sleep.

CHAPTER TWO

Daybreak

Shortly before daylight, she heard the owl again. A shiver ran down her spine. She pulled the covers closer about her. In spite of her fear, she muttered, "Old foolishness."

The fire was blazing brightly. Luke must be up and gone. It was sun-up already. Quickly, she got out of bed. Her bare toes curled back from the cold, plank floor. Again, a shiver ran down her back. "Silly old woman!" she said out loud. There was no sign of Luke, and it looked to be a good day.

"There's no use wastin' time," she thought. She started cooking a pot of thin mush and brushed the hearth. Ben and Mary, both awake, sat with matted hair and shining, bright blue eyes, waiting for their breakfast. They were well-mannered youngsters and knew to be patient with Gramma, who moved as fast as she could.

Since Lizabeth's death with the baby, Ben, a natural clown, and Mary provided Luke with a lot of love. Both were loving children, and they provided entertainment for the family. Neither Ben nor Mary remembered their mother. So Gramma and Sarah were substitute mothers—not that either of them minded.

There were potatoes in the coals, and she raked one out carefully. One could not be too careful with hot coals in a wooden building. If the floor caught fire . . . well, Gramma didn't want to think of that. Instead, she fantasized about the fish that Nathan would catch and how good they would taste instead of just potatoes and mush. If they were careful, the corn would hold out until the new crop came in. They would have to piece it out with whatever they could find in the woods. She shivered again. "Somebody's a-walkin' over my grave," she muttered.

"Well, they'll just have to walk." She shrugged off the bad feeling as she got the old bucket off the shelf. She started down to the stream for water, thinking, "It's time to get the soap goin'."

Uneasily, she looked about her as she walked down the hill. She heard the owl again. It was now broad daylight, and owls don't hoot in broad daylight. "Maybe he got his time mixed up," she thought.

When she came back from the stream, the children were sitting on the stoop with their bowls of mush. They were the picture of innocence.

"It's a pretty day, Gramma," said Sarah. "I guess the dandelions are sleepin' under the leaves, just waitin' to be picked. Soon's I finish this and clean up the dishes, I'll go and see if I can find a mess. I can taste 'em already."

"Our bodies need greens," Gramma replied.

"Pa said for me to try to get some fish," said Nathan. "I'll get you some wood chopped up, Gramma, and then go down to the creek. You get the big, black iron skillet out, 'cause were goin' to feast today. I can feel it in my bones," Nathan teased.

Gramma was well pleased with Sarah and Nathan. At fourteen and almost a woman, Sarah was Gramma's best help. She looked like her mother, Lizabeth. Deep blue eyes and flaxen hair, tall and thin. Gramma saw a real beauty in Sarah.

Nathan was almost thirteen, but he was taking on the work of a man. He was short and stocky, much like Gramma was. He would grow into manhood being of average height and broad shoulders. Gramma knew he came from good stock and would become a fine, responsible man. He was already doing tasks that were meant for adults. But as times were, he had to.

"I feel something in my bones, too," said Gramma. "You all stay close to the cabin. Don't know what it is, but somethin's not right. Your Pa has gone for meat. You get your faces washed and get your work done. Nathan, you go to the creek, but keep a sharp eye out. Sarah, you go up behind the cabin for greens, but stay close. Don't know what it is, but somethin' in my bones says there's somethin' in the air that ain't right." She went into the cabin to dress the young'uns and finish her chores before she started making soap. She needed to get Ben and Mary playing with their homemade toys in the corner of the cabin.

Gramma put the wood ashes into the hopper, a triangle shaped wooden container used to make soap, poured water over them, and went to the creek to fill her bucket again. Nathan was half asleep against a big rock. She smiled at the sight of his gaunt body at ease, for once. "Guess he missed his mama more than he let on," she mused. Soon, all too soon, he would have to take a man's burdens on his shoulders.

She thought of Luke as she rolled her long, gray hair into a tight bun. Luke seemed crushed by Lizabeth's death. They had known each other since they were children in Pennsylvania, attending the same school and same Lutheran church. Gramma knew that Luke was grievin' every day, as was she. He had lost a wife; she had lost a daughter; they both had lost the baby.

Imagine him going out in that blizzard after they buried Lizabeth and the baby. He'd come back crippled but ready to take care of his family. One could see that he was fighting his sadness but still trying to be a good father to the rest of the children.

In her mind's eye, Gramma could see Luke and Lizabeth on their wedding day. Lizabeth was tall, blond, her clear blue eyes smiling with the joy of a new bride and the anticipation of a life with Luke. Luke was a bit awkward and ungainly, his dark hair tousled and his suit ill fitting. He wore his work boots because he had no other shoes.

Luke didn't know his heritage. He said his folks were Yankees. Gramma could see his determination, and she respected the way he worked. She knew he would care for a family. Now, Luke moved through life without the spirit he had before.

Gramma couldn't shake off the uneasiness she'd felt when she first heard the owl. Old family folklore had taught her that an owl that hoots in the daytime would bring bad luck.

What had possessed her to come to this god-forsaken wilderness? Here she was, stirring fat for the soap in a big iron kettle. She'd thought that when she'd reached this age she'd be sitting on her porch with Asa, both of them in their rocking chairs, watching their grandchildren play on the grass. Instead, Asa was gone. So were Lizabeth and the baby, and she was caring for her son-in-law and his four children. Was she feeling sorry for herself? Why couldn't she shake off these bad feelings? The children were all well, and, with Luke getting meat, they would have an ample supper. Spring was in the air, and things would be easier.

Ben and Mary were playing with some chips of wood that had fallen when Nathan had split the logs for the day's fire. Maybe later she'd see about making Mary that corn shuck doll she'd been promising her. Back in the fall, she'd put some good shucks on the shelf for it. She'd sit in the sun and let the tiredness bake out of her body while she worked on the doll.

Suddenly, she was seized by a sudden sense of danger. She stood up straight and looked around. "Hurry! Hurry into the cabin!" she cried to the two smaller children, who were at the woodpile. "Don't even stick your noses out 'less I call for you."

She turned to follow them, but in her haste she tripped over a log and fell face first to the ground. As she struggled to get up, she smelled a rank odor. She was too scared to move. The Indian was upon her before she could scream.

"Asa, I'm comin' home to you," she thought. Then, in the next instant, she felt the cold steel of the knife penetrate her body, and she slid slowly to the ground.

CHAPTER THREE

A Whippoorwill Sang

Smoke curled from the chimney of the log cabin, halfway up the hill from the stream where Nathan fished. It had been a hard winter, but now the joyous sounds of spring filled the air. He listened to the whippoorwill singing back there in the woods and another around the bend of the creek. Idly, Nathan wondered what they were doing singing in the daytime. They sounded glad just to be alive.

He leaned back against the sun-warmed rock and thought of how good the sun felt on his shoulders. There hadn't been much to eat since the last big snow. That's when Pa's foot got frostbitten so bad that he couldn't go to hunt until now. He'd been gone since early morning, and Nathan's mouth watered as he thought about the taste of the fresh venison Pa'd be bringing home. A growing boy couldn't fill up right on old potatoes and mush. It was made thin, to stretch out the cornmeal so it would last until they could raise another crop of corn. Pa said they had to save corn for seed, even if they starved a bit.

Nathan watched the corncob bobber float lazily on the water. Fish would help fill his emptiness. He licked his lips and thought about the fish sizzling in the big, black iron skillet. He had carried that heavy iron skillet on his back across the mountains. It would soon be filled with fish, if Nathan had any luck.

Thoughts began to creep into Nathan's mind. He was over a year younger than Sarah, but he felt like he was treated much younger. No, that wasn't right. Sometimes he was treated like a child and other times he was expected to work like an adult. He was a little perturbed with Sarah. She seemed to get all the privileges, even though there weren't many. But she and Gramma had a special relationship, while Nathan and Luke's relationship was distant. He didn't understand his father's aloofness or his background. His father would only say his background was "Yankee." Nathan didn't understand what a Yankee was.

Gramma had sent Sarah into the woods behind the cabin to hunt the new dandelions under the leaves. Nathan's stomach growled as he thought of eating a mess of greens with fish. Maybe there'd even be enough meal so Gramma would fry up some corncakes to go with supper. Maybe that was expecting too much. He'd be satisfied with the fish and the greens.

"I'd better catch that fish 'fore I go to eatin' it," he laughed to himself. He hoped there'd be enough so that he could eat until he couldn't eat another bite. It had been a long time since anyone in the family had a full skin. He didn't see how Gramma kept going. She ate less and less and even gave part of her food to the little ones. She said they needed it to keep up their strength, since they too had the fever that took Ma and the baby. Maybe if they hadn't died, Pa wouldn't have gone off into the woods and got caught in the blizzard and froze his foot. Well, the foot was better now, but it made Pa walk with a slight limp.

Nathan sat up quickly when he saw his bobber go under the water and then pop up again. Something was after the bait. A bite! A good-sized fish was on the line. He waited until the fish was hooked, then he pulled up his pole. It was a keeper and a good start on supper tonight. The whippoorwill sang again as Nathan went to the base of the big oak tree. "He's telling me there's more where that one came from," Nathan chuckled to himself. He crouched behind the tree, looking for the end of a grapevine he could use to string the fish.

As he cut off a good length of it, he felt a prickle of uneasiness that made him shudder. "Somebody's walking across my grave!" He used Gramma's expression. He tried to shrug off the uneasy feeling as he carefully threaded the vine through the gill of the glistening bass. There was the whippoorwill again. It sounded closer to the cabin. The hairs on the back of Nathan's neck rose as he began to bait his hook. "Whee! I've got the whimwhams today!" he thought.

Suddenly, the peace and quiet was shattered by the yelp of the dog. Screams of terror split the air, and the high-pitched gabble of Indians filled his eardrums. He stood for a minute, too shocked to move. There hadn't been any sign of Indians thereabouts for over a year.

He couldn't move. He had to get to the cabin to help Gramma and Mary and little Ben, but his feet seemed rooted to the ground. At last, he grabbed the old gun that Pa had told him to always carry, and he raced up the hill, reaching the clearing just in time to see the cabin burst into flames and an Indian run out the door. In his arms he carried what looked like a bundle of rags. He held it up, and Nathan could see the limpness of it as the Indian carelessly flung it aside. It was one of the children! He could see Gramma lying near the ash hopper.

In his rage, he stumbled into the clearing and fired a shot at the Indian. He missed and stopped to reload. As he knelt, he saw the Indian draw his knife and run toward him. Nathan had no time to reload his weapon but swung it at the Indian, hitting him in the arm so he dropped his knife. Nathan felt the strong arms, like iron bands, wrap around his chest. He felt his breath being squeezed from his body. As he lost consciousness, he realized that what he had heard wasn't a whippoorwill at all.

CHAPTER FOUR

Hogtied

Nathan was face down in the grass when regained consciousness. He started to get up but found his arms tied together with leather thongs and his legs lashed together. He looked around and saw no one near him. He rolled over on his back.

"Gramma, Gramma," Nathan shouted.

"Gramma, Sarah," he called again.

There was nothing but silence in the forest. The sun shone down on him and all seemed peaceful, except he couldn't move. What would he do now? He tried to sit up but couldn't.

"Gramma, help me. Sarah, where are you?"

He could hear nothing, and fear began to rise up in him. Was he going to die tied up like this? He couldn't walk and could barely crawl on his stomach. He had better inch his way to the cabin.

He was on his stomach, working his way up the hill, when suddenly he was jerked to his feet.

"Whoa, what's happenin' to me?" He said to no one.

The big Indian untied his feet and tied the rawhide strip to his wrists. Then, pointing to the woods, the Indian said, "Come."

Nathan asked, "You mean go?"

"Yes," said the Indian. "Go," as he gestured to another Indian. The second Indian, who stood at the edge of the forest, turned and started into the woods. Nathan had no other choice but to follow the lead

Indian. The second Indian kept him reminded that he was a captive by tugging at his bonds. Nathan stumbled along between the pair of braves.

Nathan's embarrassment turned to anger. He was embarrassed because he would be regarded by Luke, Gramma and Sarah as a little kid who couldn't take care of himself and got captured. Gramma and Pa wouldn't say much, but Sarah would be smug. She was into her growth spurt and was taller than Nathan now. Last year they had been the same size. He was getting stronger and broader in the shoulders, but he was younger and shorter. "And now," he thought, "captured by the Indians, as well."

They had pushed through the woods for better than an hour when they stopped to rest.

"Name?" the Indian said to Nathan.

"Nathan. What's your name?"

The Indian didn't answer but said something to the other brave that Nathan didn't understand.

"Nay?" the Indian asked.

"Nathan, Nathan." He replied.

The Indian said something more to the brave, and they started through the forest again.

Nathan watched the brave in front of him. He seemed younger than the Indian who had tied him up. The Indians seemed to be a year or so older than Nathan and weren't hostile to him at all. The Indian leading him seemed to be more interested in tracking through the forest than taking care of Nathan. Maybe he was a young buck learning how to find his way home. The older Indian never gave him directions, as far as Nathan could figure.

"I'm thirsty," Nathan said.

"No water here," the Indian replied.

"Where is the water?" Nathan asked.

"No water here," the Indian said again.

Once again, Nathan's dark thoughts turned inward. Embarrassed, angry, and now he was afraid for his life. Would the Indians kill him? Would he become their slave? How would he escape? Would Pa come a-looking? How did this happen? It started out as a nice, warm, normal spring day. What had happened?

The Indians slowed up and came into a small clearing with a cave off to the side. The Indian motioned for Nathan to sit, and he re-tied Nathan's feet. Nathan's arms hurt from being tied behind his back, and sitting on the ground all tied up was not much better. What would happen next?

CHAPTER FIVE

A Mess of Greens

Sarah climbed the steep hill behind the cabin. Her feet shuffled through the limp, damp leaves. In her basket she had yellow-green dandelions, the first of the spring, that she had found hidden under the leaves. They would cook up into a tasty mess of greens to eat with the fish that Nathan was bound to catch. She was hungry. The thought of the roasting meat that Pa would bring from hunting made her cravings even greater.

There'd been little enough food to go around the past winter. Because of the blizzard, Pa's hurt foot had kept him homebound, and the starving animals that were always around the cabin waited for a chance to steal whatever food they could. Well, spring was here, and Pa and Nathan would soon plant corn seed. Pa could hunt again, and there would be berries, and greens in the woods to eat until the corn was ripe. It was good to be alive.

She bent to cut some more dandelions. They were so lacy-looking. It took a good many to fill a pot. It looked as though she had pretty well covered this side of the hill, but she still didn't have enough greens. There had been no sign of Indians for a long time, so she felt safe in going to the other side of the hill. Pa would tan her good if he ever knew that she had wandered so far from the cabin alone. She'd be careful; the lure of finding enough greens so that she could eat until she hurt was more powerful than the fear that Pa might be angry with her. After all, she was certainly able to take care of herself.

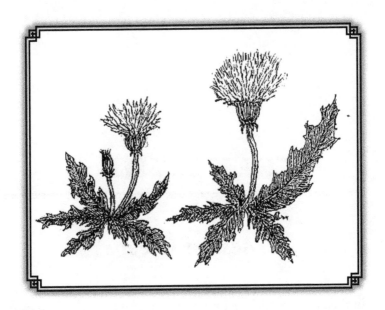

The greens on the far side of the hill seemed twice as big as those on the other side of the hill. Quickly, she dropped to her hands and knees and began to cut the tender young shoots. They were so thick in this patch that she soon filled the basket. She stood up and brushed the wet leaves from her knees. Slowly, she picked up her basket and began to walk back home.

The chattering of a squirrel, a sudden whirring sound, and a bright flash of movement startled her so much that she dropped her basket. "Drat! That bird sure gave me a fright!" she thought as she stooped to gather the spilled greens. "I'd better hurry so as not to worry Gramma. No tellin' how long I've been away."

It was much harder going up the hill with a full basket than it was going down. She didn't realize that she had wandered so far. The basket seemed to get heavier and heavier. Would she ever get to the top of the hill? She must have been gone even longer than she thought. It was getting chilly, and she could see the graying sky through the tops of the trees.

The scolding of an angry squirrel startled her. She stumbled over a root, righted herself, and tugged her basket higher on her arm. While she was fourteen, she was still a young girl—and she was much too young to be in the woods by herself. Her faded dress barely had any color left, and her long, thin legs were briar-scratched and mud-streaked. Her bright blue eyes seemed sad, and her blond curls were in need of some attention. Her skirt caught on a branch. With an impatient tug, she tore it loose. Gramma would be angry about that. "Lord knows, it's hard enough to keep up with the cookin' and cleanin' up after you young'uns without me havin' to mend for you, too," she'd chide. "What with your ma gone, and havin' little enough to do with, it plumb wears a body down," Sarah could hear her say.

Gramma had fussed a lot lately about things that didn't count. She never used to be that way. Dimly, Sarah could remember how Gramma had kept up with Ma and Pa on the long trip over the mountains when they came into Kentucky from their old homestead in Pennsylvania. Sarah couldn't remember much about living there. About all she could recall of the journey was being half-hungry all of the time and having Pa carry her over the hard places. That sure had been nice. She thought how she had snuggled her nose in the warm place in his neck, just below where his beard ended. She also remembered Pa telling her that over the next hills was the "Promised Land," where streams ran with milk and honey. "Glory Land," he'd called it. "Well," she said aloud, "There sure ain't been any milk or honey or much of anything else to eat lately. If I don't get home soon, Gramma won't have time to cook these greens today."

The squirrel, nearer now, seemed to be telling her, too, to hurry. There was a clear place ahead, and she could make better time. My, those briars stung. She wished the old squirrel would be quiet. She was beginning to feel uneasy. She knew she had to hurry. He seemed to be fussing at her just like Gramma would when she got back to the cabin. She reached the clearing and began to run. She slipped on some wet leaves and spilled greens from her basket again. There wasn't time to pick them up this time, as she was beginning to panic. She had to get home. Anxiously, she looked behind her as she reached the top of the hill. In a few minutes, she would be safe inside the cabin. The squirrel chattered right in front of her now. Again, she looked back. She turned to run but was stopped in her tracks by the greased, painted body of an Indian. The sound of the chattering squirrel came from his mouth. She screamed only once. The basket fell from her arm and slowly rolled down the hill.

CHAPTER SIX

A Long Way to the Licks

Luke had wakened long before daybreak. Carefully, so as not to disturb the sleeping boy on the pallet next to his, he reached for his moccasins. He pulled them on his feet, wincing slightly as the cold leather pulled against the tender skin of the foot that had been frostbitten. It still gave him trouble and would slow him down from the usual pace that he set for himself when hunting. There was no way out of it. He couldn't wait any longer. He'd just have to worry over his slowness and favor the foot. They had to have meat.

Stiffly, he climbed down the ladder. He went to the fire and poked at the black log. On the table lay the food that Gramma had prepared for him to take. He looked over at her in the bed with Sarah. She looked so small; a breeze could blow her away. She was plumb wore out, what with nursing Lizabeth and Beth and the little ones, not to mention himself when he'd come home from the woods with his foot hurting so. She'd been so brave during the hard winter. It was no wonder she was so fretful now.

He remembered that she'd never asked to rest during the long trek over the mountains three years ago, though he could see she was worn to the very marrow of her bones. Hers was the spirit that would make this country great.

He looked at the food on the trestle table he had made. He had built it from a pine tree cleared from the field where the first crop of corn had been grown the first year. Settlers had agreed to raise a crop and build a permanent structure in order to lay claim to the free land.

Luke, with help from Lizabeth, had built the cabin and a makeshift stick-and-mud chimney. The clearing and planting took up most of their time and strength. The next year, he had built a sled. With the help of Nathan, he had hauled rocks on it from the stream and made a good, stone chimney. The stone chimney was the centerpiece of their cabin, and it would last through several lifetimes. He had floored the loft with rough boards for the children to sleep on, and last year he had put a floor in the cabin; Lizabeth was so pleased with having a wooden floor instead of the packed dirt floor.

She had many of Gramma's ways. She liked to keep things tidy. Every day, she sprinkled the floor with sand and swept it clean with her rush broom, so that now the rough places in the boards were worn smooth. He had promised Lizabeth that next year he would build a dog-trot and connect a second cabin to the one in which they lived. The family was growing, and they needed more room. Sarah, Nathan, Ben and Mary were crowded into the loft. Gramma's bed occupied one corner of the cabin, and their bed took up another. There was no room for a cradle, so the baby slept between them. Now that Lizabeth and the baby were dead, what they had would do for the time being.

At this time, he was concerned only about food for the family. Soon, he would have to sow the seed for the corn crop. He remembered how Lizabeth had liked walking behind him dropping corn as he dug the rows. He shrugged off the feeling of loss, even though the pain was severe. He had to concentrate on getting meat for the family, and daylight wasn't far off.

It would be cold in the woods until the sun came up. He took his buckskin shirt off the peg and pulled it over his head. He'd better make tracks so he wouldn't be gone too long. He'd hoped he didn't have to go clear to the licks. He didn't like having to go so far from the place. Things had been peaceful thereabouts for a while, but the settlers never knew when the Indians would rise up and cause trouble.

At the moment, the Shawnees up around a place called Chillicothe had been pretty quiet since Tecumseh had become their leader. Luke didn't feel there was much to worry about as long as he was their chief. Of course, there were always those hostile, renegade bands that would raid and steal anything and everything from unprotected settlers. They were a worry.

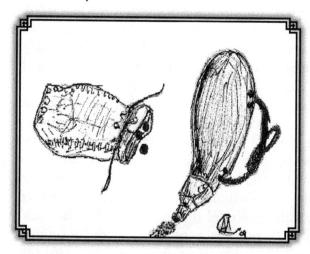

On the table he laid the fishhooks he had fashioned for Nathan to use. He should catch some fish today. They would taste mighty good to the family.

Luke slung the shot pouch and powder horn over his shoulder. He put the packet of jerky in the front of his shirt and picked up his rifle. He pulled the heavy door closed behind him. He stood for a moment on the flat rock the children called the stoop and looked around. For some reason, he was slow about getting started this morning.

There was a faint glow of pink in the eastern sky that warned him that he must be on his way. He shrugged off his uneasiness to go and began the loose, steady pace that would enable him to cover miles without becoming tired.

He was alert to everything about him. His eyes moved constantly from one side to the other. Even a bent twig had meaning for him. He could tell from the looks of a track how long it had been since the animal that made it had crossed that place. His were the ways of the woodsman.

He traveled at an even rate until the sun was straight overhead. Only then did he allow himself to stop and rest for a while. He drank from a clear spring and pulled a piece of jerky from his poke. Leaning against a tree, Luke chewed on a piece of stringy meat and let his thoughts wander.

Sometimes he was half sorry they had left the farm in Pennsylvania. He had owned a nice house and good farm land. All his folks and Lizabeth's Pa, Asa, were buried there. They were buried in the old Lutheran churchyard. It was Luke that wanted to move. He wanted more farmland for himself and his growing family. The farm in Pennsylvania was too small to include two sons and maybe some sons-in-law. When he heard the land across the Alleghenies was there for the picking, he decided to go west. He knew that with the sweat of his brow and hard work he could make a farmstead for his family. He knew it would be hard, but the land would be free and clear. Together, he and Lizabeth would make a new home. He had made up his mind.

They sold everything but what they could carry on their backs and pack on the mare. It was hard to part with many of the things they couldn't carry. He remembered Gramma turning her head to hide the tears in her eyes when he took down the clock that had sat on the mantle ever since she and her husband, Asa, had put it there when they first set up housekeeping. Yes, Gramma had grit. He hadn't considered that she would come with them until she announced that she wasn't staying behind, nor was she going back east to live with her brother. She was coming to Kentucky. It was probably the only way she'd ever get to the "Promised Land," she had laughed. Now he didn't know how he'd have made out if it hadn't been for her.

He thought about Sarah. She was beginning to look like her mother and act like her grandmother. That wasn't a bad combination. He shook off his memories.

Time to get moving again. He wanted to get to the salt lick before sundown, when the animals gather there. He was hoping to get a good-sized buck in the morning.

As he neared the lick, he circled around so that he would be downwind from it. Cautiously, he moved closer. He made no sound as he crept through the woods. He waited patiently until three does and a buck came into view. He controlled his breathing and made no movement. He knew that deer couldn't see color, but any movement would spook them. He watched the buck and thought, "Closer, closer."

He knew he had one shot. There would be no time to reload. The deer would be over the next hill before he could reload, and the report from the old muzzle-loader would scare every deer within five miles. He had to be certain. He waited and waited. "Steady," he said to himself.

Now, taking careful aim, he fired the flintlock and dropped the buck. It was a clean kill. He hurried down to the deer and cut his throat to bleed him out.

Swiftly, since it was becoming dark, he slit the carcass, cleaned out the innards, tied a rope to the antlers, and hung the carcass on a branch. He needed to get the deer high enough so predators wouldn't try to get the meat.

Exhausted, he built a fire and stuck strips of liver on the sticks to roast. The liver was very tasty, and Luke knew it wouldn't keep on the trip home. He ate his fill and dropped off into a very heavy sleep.

As soon as it was light enough to see, he cut the deer down the middle so he could fashion two packs that he could carry. He cut a chunk of salt from the lick and added it to the pack. It would help preserve the meat, and the family could always use salt.

It would take him twice as long to get home, since he would have to carry one pack for a ways then leave it hanging from a tree and go back and get the other one. Not only would it take him twice as long but also he would use up twice as much energy. He had made it to the lick in one day. He figured it would take him two days to get back home. That would be a total of three days. It couldn't be helped. He had got the deer. His hungry family could eat well.

He picked up the largest pack after he had tied the other high in the branches of the tree. As he settled the pack securely on his shoulders, he felt uneasy. He looked around. It was almost as though there was someone behind him. "Never had feelings like that before," he said aloud. "Guess I've been living in the past too much lately."

Luke was tired but anxious to get home. It was near the end of the third day since he had left. He didn't have far to go. He had seen no signs of Indians to report to his family. "Guess ole Tecumseh is doin' a good job," he thought as he stepped up his pace. He was eager to see the faces of the children when he showed them the meat. What a feast they would have! Gramma would be fussing around like an old brood hen trying to decide what to cook up first. At last, he'd sit at his own table and watch them eat their fill.

He'd hurry home with this pack and go back first thing in the morning for the other. Maybe he'd even take Nathan with him. It looked quiet enough about so that they could both leave the cabin.

As he started toward the last ridge he could see plumes of smoke rising from the clearing. "Looks like Gramma has the fire going ready for the deer that I'm bringin' in," he thought.

"She's probably got the stew pot out just waitin' to add the meat."

He came over the top of the ridge and stopped dead in his tracks. There before him were the smoking ruins of the cabin. He stood stock still, staring in horror. His mind was unable to comprehend. He stood as though he had turned to stone.

Unnoticed, the pack of meat slid from his shoulders as he dropped to his knees and cried, "No! God, no!"

CHAPTER SEVEN

The Promise

Luke stepped back from the graves he had just dug. Aloud he said, "Lizabeth, you and the baby are not alone. These loved ones have joined you. I failed to protect them and I failed you."

He sat on the stoop, with only the stone chimney rising behind him, put his head down, and sobbed. The ashes were all that was left of the house. He stared at the new graves and tried to speak again but all he could say was, "Lizabeth, I'm sorry."

Slowly, the realization came to him that Nathan and Sarah were not there. Where were they? And why hadn't he thought of them sooner? They might be hiding out in the woods somewhere. He had to find them. He must force himself to think.

The ashes looked to be three days old. The Indians must have raided the day he left. Nathan had been going to fish, so he started toward the stream. Luke was afraid of what he would find. Like a very old, defeated man, he got to his feet. What a fool he was for leaving them! He'd thought they'd be safe, because there hadn't been any trouble from the Indians for so long. Why hadn't he paid more attention to Gramma and her feelings of foreboding? If he had been there, maybe he could have held off the attack. If not, he'd have gone with them. That would have been better than this.

Now he would have to find Nathan and Sarah and do what had to be done. Then he'd leave this place forever. He wished with all his heart that he had never heard of Kentucky.

With dragging steps, he forced himself past the overturned kettle. Slowly, he started across the clearing. He turned his head so as not to see the three new mounds of dirt.

For the first time in his life, he was careless in the woods as he headed toward the stream. He'd even forgotten about his rifle, left where he had dropped it on the hill when he saw the cabin. All he could think about was what he had to do before he could leave.

He reached the rock where Nathan fished. He saw where he had gone to the tree and found the pole leaning against it. There was a grapevine that he used for a stringer with the remains of a fish still attached. There was no sign of Nathan or of a struggle. Then Luke saw the tracks that showed Nathan running toward the clearing. He followed them to the place where Nathan had dropped the gun. It was gone. The ground showed scuffling marks. Hopefully, Luke realized that Nathan might have been taken alive. At least he was alive when he left the clearing. The tracks clearly showed that he had been able to walk. He had not been alone. Shawnee tracks partly covered his. A captive! Nathan had been captured. He might still be alive.

Luke knew that the Indians often took captives for slaves, especially when they were young and healthy, like Nathan. He was almost thirteen years old. It was a good age for the Indians to train him in Indian ways. They took girls, too. But they wanted the girls for their wives. The Shawnee did not object to mixing white blood with theirs. In fact, there were many of them who had French blood running through their veins.

Hope rose in Luke. Maybe Sarah had been captured, too. The life of a slave was miserable, but it was better than no life at all. As the ability to reason returned to Luke, he knew that he had to get his rifle before he could do anything else. He must use every caution because he must save his children. He couldn't help them if he were captured or killed.

He found his rifle where he had dropped it. He went back to the cabin. There was no sign that Sarah had been there when Gramma was attacked. The Indians had disposed of the little ones because they were too much bother to take back. The Indians needed to move quickly, and the babies would have slowed them down. Where was Sarah?

Luke tried to think back to what might have happened to Sarah on the day he left. Normally, Sarah would have been there helping

Gramma. She wouldn't have gone far from the cabin. She never went off except to go a little piece into the woods behind the cabin. Usually he or Nathan went with her. Then he remembered Gramma talking about greens. Sarah must have gone to find dandelions to cook with the fish, he decided.

He started through the trees. Soon, he found the place where she had pushed aside leaves and cut the plants. He followed her trail until he came to a bush where a piece of cloth torn from Sarah's dress still hung. A few yards beyond that lay the basket. A trail of wilted greens led him to the place where Sarah had stopped. He saw the moccasin print and knew that Sarah had been captured as well.

Grimly, Luke set his lips. He knew now what he had to do. "Lizabeth, I promise you that I will get them both back safe. I won't fail you again," he vowed aloud. Tears of grief and bitterness streamed down his cheeks.

CHAPTER EIGHT

A Meeting at the Cave

Sarah thought that the Indian would never stop. They had been moving constantly since they left the hill. Her wrists hurt where the rawhide thong cut into her flesh as he pulled her along. When she stumbled, he'd jerk the strap until it felt as though her arms would be yanked clear off her body. The bushes slapped and clawed at her. At first, she had been too scared to even notice them. Now her body felt like one big welt. She tried to avoid the sharp stings, but she couldn't always see the branches in time.

She kept her eyes fastened on the brown figure ahead of her who kept her at such a constant pace. The Indian wore only a breechcloth, and his coarse, black hair was parted down the middle and tied on each side with strings of deer hide just below his ears. She could smell that his body had been greased with bear fat. It was a very pungent odor. It wasn't fresh bear fat either, she thought.

As though the savage could read her mind and didn't like her thoughts, he jerked the line to make the girl move faster.

"I'll show him!" she thought as she stumbled along after him. The Indian moved soundlessly through the underbrush. Sarah made as much noise as though she were driving cattle.

They kept on traveling until mid-afternoon when they reached a small cave near the stream they had followed for some time. The Indian pushed Sarah into the cave and tied the thong to a rock that jutted out from the wall.

The Indian glared at Sarah and said, "Stay." Ducking his head at the entrance, he went out. Sarah was so tired that she lay down where she had fallen. She hardly noticed that he had gone. After she had rested, she began to think. What would Gramma do when Sarah didn't come home? She would be very worried. She wouldn't know that Sarah had been so foolish and gone so far from the cabin. Poor Gramma. She'd be half out of her mind with worry. How could she know there had been an Indian in the woods?

Sarah began to wonder where the Indian had gone. Afraid to be with him, she was more afraid to be alone. Suppose he'd gone off and left her tied to the rock? Maybe some wild animal would get her, or she might starve. She didn't like the way the Indian looked, or the way he smelled, or the way he had pulled her along, but she wished he would come back.

What she really wished was that Pa'd walk though that opening. Pa! What would he say when he found out that she had disobeyed Gramma and gone to the other side of the big hill? He'd sure be upset with her for not doing what she was told. Why had she been so greedy for more greens?

Greens! Sarah wished she had some now. She was so hungry she could eat them raw. "I wonder how many fish Nathan caught," she pondered.

Her stomach growled with emptiness. It seemed that she could smell the fish cooking right now. When she shut her eyes and thought about the crisp skin and flaky white meat of the fish, she could almost taste it. Maybe if she kept her eyes shut, she could pretend she was eating fish. The smell was even stronger. It was almost as though the fish were right in front of her. Sarah sighed and rolled over. It was no use pretending. It just made her hungrier. As tired as she was, she fell into a deep sleep.

"Don't!" Sarah muttered as she felt her shoulder being shaken, "Let me be. I'm too tired to get up yet, Gramma."

Slowly, she began to waken. It was cold and she was hungry. She was still in the cave. Being home had been a dream. Still, she smelled cooked fish. Unwillingly, Sarah opened her eyes. She blinked. Surely, this, too, was a dream. She couldn't believe her eyes. There before her on the floor of the cave was a steaming, fresh-cooked fish. With grimy hands, the starving girl snatched at it, pulled off a large chunk and stuffed it into her mouth. Never had anything tasted so good. Sarah tore at the fish until there was nothing left of it. Finally, she sat back and wiped her hands on her torn skirt. Only then did she notice that she was no longer tied.

Awareness came back to her, and she realized that the Indian must have untied her while he caught the fish and then cooked it. He was not going to let her starve, after all. It certainly made her feel better since she had eaten. Now she must think. Never had she been so frightened that she was unable to think. What could she do? Escape! Pa would escape. Then so would she.

The entrance of the cave was ahead of her. She jumped to her feet and started toward it. Somehow she would find her way home.

Just as she reached the opening, it darkened. The big body of the Indian blocked out the light and stopped her from going any farther. From behind him, she heard the guttural voices of other Indians. As she slipped to the ground, into unconsciousness, she heard her name being called.

CHAPTER NINE

Another Promise

"Sarah! Sarah! Wake up!!" She was being shaken so hard that her head rolled from side to side. She didn't want to wake up. She wanted to stay in the safe darkness that held no Indians, no terror. The voice wouldn't let her be. "Sarah! Sarah!" It was pulling her back to consciousness. Dimly she realized that it was a voice she knew.

A smart slap across her cheek stung her. "Don't hurt me," she said weakly and began to cry.

"Sarah! Sarah! You must wake up!" Lightly she was slapped again.

Nathan! Nathan! It was Nathan! What was he doing here? Now fully awake, she sat up quickly.

"Did you come to save me, Nathan? How did you ever find me? Did Gramma send you? Is she very put out with me for wandering so far? I guess she was really worried when I didn't come back. Oh, Nathan, I am so glad you found me!" Sarah was so happy to see Nathan that she chattered on without thinking. Suddenly she stopped talking as she realized that they were still in the cave. She didn't like being there.

"Sarah, are you all right? The Indians didn't hurt you, did they?" he asked.

"No, only my legs and arms sting where the bushes scratched me. We went so fast that I had a stitch in my side, but that's gone now. Did Gramma send you after me? Was she awful mad at me? I 'spect she was half out of her mind when I didn't come home. Poor Gramma," she sighed.

"Sarah, listen to me," Nathan put up his hand to stop her talking.

She raised her head and looked him full in the face. She opened her mouth to speak again but stopped before a sound came out. Her eyes opened wider and wider as she heard voices outside the cave. They said Indian words. Then she knew that Nathan, too, had been captured.

Her shoulders slumped. Without knowing what she was doing, she began pulling threads from the torn place on her dress and rolling them into tight little balls between her fingers. She didn't want to think. Nathan was talking to her, but she didn't want to listen.

Finally some of his words pierced her unwillingness. "Ben! Mary! Fire! Gramma!" What was he saying? She began to listen as Nathan told her about the Indian raid on the cabin. Nathan wasn't sure but he thought that Gamma and one of the little children might have been hurt or worse. He didn't know what happened to the other child. The cabin was on fire.

Tears of worry and anger rolled down her cheeks as she heard what might have happened to Gramma and the little children. "What would Pa find when he got home and they were all gone?" she asked herself.

"Sarah," Nathan got her attention again. "We've got to make a plan. We've got to get back to Pa."

"Escape! Nathan was thinking just like Pa," she thought. She wiped her grimy face with the hem of her dress. "What can we do? How can we get away?" she asked.

"I don't know yet. All I know is these Indians are Shawnee so we are lucky. Shawnees don't torture prisoners. Shooting Star is the big chief. Think Pa said his name was Tecumseh. Pa says he's a good Indian as Indians go. He's tryin' to help his people."

"Humph!" Sarah snorted. "Gramma says that the only good Indian is a dead 'un. From the way they smell, I'd say that she's right."

"Sarah, you watch your mouth. Some of these Indians know a little English. You don't want to make them mad at us. Besides, there are many good Indians around. You keep your feelings to yourself and don't go spoutin' off about anything like you was at home." Nathan cautioned her.

He silenced her for a while and she sat thinking. "What do you think they'll do with us?" She was beginning to be afraid again. There was no telling what the Indians had planned. Well, for one thing, they won't do anything until daylight. They ain't movin' at night. It ain't their nature.

"At daylight, what then?" Sarah interrupted. Now she didn't want to think of leaving the comfort of the cave.

Nathan thought for a while. Finally, he said, "It's my guess they'll take us to one of their camps. They'll probably make us slaves. You'll live in one of the quonsets and work for the wives. They will give you all the jobs they don't want to do, and they will teach you their ways. Then a brave will select you as a wife and . . ."

Nathan got no farther. "One of his wives?" Sarah gasped. "Marry! I'd rather die first."

"Shhh! Sarah! I told you to watch your mouth. That ain't goin' to happen. We're goin' to get away. And don't tempt an Indian to kill ya, 'cause they will."

"But how will we escape?"

"I don't know yet. Let me study on it. We'd better get some sleep. No tellin' how far they'll travel tomorrow. We need rest."

"Nathan, I'm powerful scared." Sarah murmured as she lay down on the hard rock floor of the cave. "I want to go home."

"I'm here, Sarah. I'll take care of you as best I can." Nathan lay down beside her and put his arm over her.

Like the two tired children they were, they quickly dropped off into a deep sleep.

In his sleep, Nathan muttered, "I'll take care of you, Sarah, I will."

At sun-up they were awakened by moccasined feet poking at them. Grunting and pointing, the Indians showed them they were heading north. The savage who had captured Sarah picked up the thong and tied it around her wrists. She pulled back as he picked up the other end of it. "Go now," the Indian said.

Then he grinned at the other Indians and boasted proudly, "This one, she mine," as he started off into the forest pulling Sarah as he went.

Again, Sarah became overwhelmed with fear as she stumbled after him. She begged half out loud, "Oh, God, please help me."

CHAPTER TEN

A Call for Help

Luke stumbled into the stockade. His eyes were feverish and he swayed with fatigue. "Indians!" he cried hoarsely. "Indians!"

Quickly, a crowd gathered around him. "Indians!" the word spread like wildfire through the camp. There'd been no sign of Indians for so long that the people had begun to feel safe. They had become careless. Now mothers gathered their children close to them and men looked to their rifles. Uneasiness hung over all of them.

Most of the people at the fort were newly arrived in Kentucky. They had been lured here by the essays of men like Gilbert Imlay and Bernard Mayo, who wrote stories of the beauty of the land and how it was called *"The Goshen of the West."* The newer arrivals hadn't yet felt the threat of the Indians, who resented the white man coming into their land and plowing up their hunting grounds. Now, settlers were forced to face the Indian resentment. A cabin had been raided. A woman and two children were dead. Two other children were kidnapped. Fear was in the air.

The men moved closer to their families. Soon, they planned to leave the safety of the fort. They planned to go into the wilderness to homestead land, build their cabins and clear the land. They would be leaving the protection of the garrison at the fort and going off alone. They worried about leaving their wives and children alone, as they would have to hunt for meat and go for supplies. This tragedy could happen to them, too.

A big man pushed his way through the crowd around Luke. "What's this about an attack?" he asked. "There ain't been no Indian sign since the winter before last."

With pain, Luke began to tell his story. When he got to the part where the signs showed that Sarah had been captured, he completely broke down. His children were out there somewhere, prisoners of the Indians. "No tellin' what's happened to them," he sobbed.

"What tribe were they, Luke?" one man asked.

"Looked to be Shawnees. Could be it's a renegade group or maybe another tribe tryin' to look Shawnee. Don't ever really know with Indians. I just pray it *is* Shawnees. They're more decent than other Indians around. If it's Shawnee, they'll be headin' north to one of their settlements on the big river, or they may be goin' to a place they call Chillicothe. I don't rightly know. All I know is that all signs point north. I'll go alone for my young'uns if I have to, but I'd sure appreciate some help in gettin' 'em back. I know Nathan and Sarah are with the Indians. Don't know if they'll end up at the same place or not. Gramma and the two little ones are gone. Guess the Indians figured Gramma was too old and slow and the little ones too much of a bother to make the trip. Looks to me like the Indians are goin' a long way; otherwise they would have taken the two little ones." Luke reasoned.

"How far did you follow the trail?" Sam Stewart asked.

"I went up to where the stream forks over the ridge four, five miles from here when I followed Nathan's trail. On Sarah's, they went toward the main rise. They went in two different ways. Had to be the same tribe, but don't know if they'll end up in the same village. That's why I need help. Time's a wastin' and I can't go two ways at once."

A trapper, Sam'l, stepped forward. "I'm with you, Luke," he said. "How many men do you reckon you'll need?"

"Two or three for each trail," Luke replied. "No men who are green to this country. Just men who can read signs and know the Indian ways."

Several men stepped forward. Luke considered them. "John, you're a good man, and I know what you are thinkin', but you ain't been here long enough to know what the signs say. You're needed at the fort in case there's a full-scale attack. You're a good shot with the rifle. Sam'l, you come along. You ain't got chick nor child to fret after you if you get took. Squire, you know more about Indian ways than any man here. I'll need you. Jason, you got the grit we need to hold to the trail. You can go longer on less than any man I've ever seen. James, I can't ask you. You've got the responsibility of the whole stockade on you. You need to be here. Lige, you can read trail better than any man I've ever hunted with. Matthew, you're the best stalker in a close place I know." One by one, Luke chose the men who would help get his children back.

There was no need to talk. Each man was a veteran of the woods. He knew what he would need and what he would have to do. Swiftly, they prepared to leave the fort. In complete unspoken agreement, they divided themselves into groups of three. Squire was acknowledged leader of one, Luke the second. Jason and Sam'l lined up with Squire, while Matthew and Lige followed Luke.

The heavy, log gate of the fort slowly swung closed behind the men. Inside, preparations were being made in case of an Indian attack. The easy-going ways were gone; each person was anxious and alert. The Indians might never come, but in case they did, the people in the fort would be ready.

The six men entered the forest, each with his own thoughts and a dedicated spirit to get the children back.

CHAPTER ELEVEN

Two Trails Meet

"Looks like they stopped here for the night, Jason. These ashes in the clearing have been cold three, four days at the most. The prints around here are the same tracks we've been seeing. Some of them are pretty scuffled, like they pow-wowed here."

"They must have spent some time here. They've been in the cave. Can't tell much about it in the dusk."

"Squire, come out of that cave and look over here. 'Pears to be another set of tracks coming in from this way."

"Yep, Sam'l. These are different from them of the Indians we've been following that took the boy."

The three men examined the trail for a short way into the woods. "Looks like just one Indian on this trail, and he had the girl. They must have planned to meet here. Luke's party should be showin' up soon, since he's on the girl's trail. That Indian sure took the long way 'round to get here."

"Funny thing, they didn't bother to cover their tracks around here. The trail was hard enough to follow from Luke's place up 'til now. Here, a baby could read the signs."

"Guess they didn't expect to be followed so soon. They probably watched the cabin before they raided and saw Luke goin' off to hunt. Indians smart as Shawnees usually study out a place before they hit it."

"They must have only gone to Luke's place, small band like this. Looks to be just five of them, from the tracks. Could be renegades, Jason."

"Could be they're meetin' up with a war party, too." Sam'l studied the tracks again.

"Yep! Might be there's raidin' parties at other outlyin' cabins like Luke's. I heard that the Shawnee had some kind of fever sickness that killed off a bunch of them. Mostly children. They might be gettin' young'uns to keep up the tribe number. They get 'em young as these of Luke's and they can pretty well train them in the Indian ways. Pretty soon the boys and girls begin thinkin' they're Shawnees instead of . . ." Squire suddenly stopped talking and raised his rifle ready to shoot.

There had been no noticeable sound from the forest, but he sensed something was there.

Silently, the men slipped to find cover. They watched as the bushes were cautiously parted. Three men came into view; Matthew and Lige closely followed by Luke stepped into the clearing. Squire walked out to meet them.

With a few words, he told Luke about finding the sets of tracks that met. Luke sighed with relief. He knew that at least Nathan and Sarah were together. They could comfort each other. It would be easier, too, just having one trail to follow. In the morning, they could start tracking again. It was too late in the day now to see well enough to read the signs.

"Ain't no need for all of us to go on," he decided. "Sam'l, if you'll come with me, the others can go back to the fort. We'll stir up a lot less fuss in the woods and can get there faster if we ain't an army."

The men accepted what he said as being practical. At daybreak they parted.

No one wished Luke and Sam'l luck. They would either rescue the children or be killed or captured themselves. All frontiersmen understood this.

CHAPTER TWELVE

Life in the Village

Sarah was terrified by the number of Indian women who gathered around her as she was shoved into the light of a huge bonfire. They poked at her with stiff fingers and grunted as they did so. They felt her blond hair and tried pulling it. She tried to stay beside Nathan, but he was soon led away. Bravely, she tried to keep back tears of rage and frustration. She stood straight and tall and held her head high. She was taller than most Indian women. If only she could rest and clean up, she could endure whatever they had in mind for her.

An older woman approached her. She scattered the women like so many chickens, and, taking Sarah not un-gently by the arm, led her to a smaller fire. There, with a gesture, she indicated that Sarah should sit on the ground. A stick hung over the fire. Spitted on it was a half-cooled animal of some sort. The Indian woman reached toward it with her hand and pulled off a piece of meat. She handed the meat to Sarah.

Sarah didn't even notice that the hand that held the meat was still unwashed from the time it had skinned that same animal. Ravenously, she pulled and tugged at the meat with her teeth while juices from it ran down her chin and stained her dirty, torn dress.

She also didn't notice that the woman had gone into the shelter they sat in front of. She returned, carrying a gourd of an astringent smelling salve. She set the gourd on the ground near Sarah.

Finally, Sarah had satisfied her hunger enough to look around. Everyone seemed busy at some task or other. There were many shelters like the one behind her, and many people seemed to belong to each shelter. Sarah was too tired to wonder much about what was happening. She slid into a curled position and cradled her head on her arms. Sleep would not be held off. Soon, a moccasin toe nudged her from slumber. She struggled to wake up. Finally, she sat up to find that the woman was handing her the gourd that contained the salve. She pointed to the salve and then to Sarah's cuts and scratches. All Sarah wanted to do was sleep. However, the woman would not leave her alone until she had smeared salve on the places that were cut. At last, having satisfied the woman's urgings, Sarah was allowed to go to sleep.

At daybreak, Sarah's arm was roughly shaken. Reluctantly, she opened her eyes to find that she was inside the hut, sleeping on a pallet of rough furs. A young woman was standing over her. Impatiently, by gestures, she indicated that Sarah was to come with her. Sore and bruised, Sarah slowly got to her feet and limped outside. The young woman attached a leather thong to one of Sarah's still raw and bleeding arms and led her to the edge of the woods. There she heaped Sarah's arms high with firewood and led her back to the camp. After several trips back and forth, Sarah was given a bone with some meat left on it. It looked like something that should have been thrown to the dogs. Sarah didn't notice. She was too hungry to care. When the meat had been eaten off the bone, Sarah was still hungry, and like a dog, she gnawed at the bone, hoping to find a shred of meat or marrow she had missed.

All day, she was led back and forth until the pile of wood she had carried was higher than she could reach. At nightfall, she was too tired to even wonder what had happened to Nathan.

Later the next day she saw him. He was with some young braves who had just come in from the hunt. She hardly recognized him, as he was covered with blood. She ran to where he stood. At his feet was a pile of small animals. His eyes met hers but warned her to say nothing. Instead, he pointed to the game and said, "Girl, skin these for your family. Come pick them up and take them to your house."

When she got close enough to hear a whisper, he said, "I'm fine, Sarah. They're takin' me on hunts. I carry back what they kill. I'm watchin' an' waitin'. If I get a chance, I'll get you away from here. Do whatever you are told. Learn everything you can about the ways of the Indians. Now go! Don't look back."

Sarah gathered the squirrels and rabbits and carried them back to the old woman, who indicated that Sarah was to skin and clean the animals. Later, she roasted them over the open fire. There was plenty of meat to eat now, but oh, how she wished for some vegetables. Perhaps she could find some greens in the woods. The fiddleneck ferns should be up by now. Maybe tomorrow, she thought, she would get a chance to look for some when she was gathering wood.

Her thoughts were interrupted by the arrival of several braves to the camp. This meant that, as a slave, Sarah would be worked much harder than usual. The men would talk far into the night, and she would have to serve them if they became thirsty or hungry. She sighed and began to build up the fire to prepare the meal for them.

The woman, Little Bird, called her from the fire. For some reason Sarah did not understand, Little Bird seemed to like Sarah. She had given Sarah salve, and now she handed Sarah several deerskins. By signs, she told Sarah that she was to make herself clothing from them.

Sarah was grateful. The clothes she had worn were tattered and filthy. Now, with help from Little Bird, she could make herself an outfit that would make her feel more like a person. At least she would be clean and wouldn't stand out as she did as a blond-haired, blue-eyed girl wearing a tattered dress. She promised herself that she would find a way to bathe before she wore any of the new clothing.

As the days passed, Sarah was given more and more freedom and more and more responsibility. She wore her outfit of skins and became more comfortable wearing it. Soon she was allowed to go to the river alone to get water in the birch pails that she had learned to make. Sarah was grateful because each time she went to the river she washed her face and hands. She was as content as she could be as a slave. She had food, decent clothing, and was as clean as she could keep herself. She had learned many useful things.

She watched Nathan for signs that he had a plan. He was often gone all day with hunting parties. He had gained the confidence of the Indians to the degree that he carried a small bow and was learning to shoot arrows from it. The young Indian boys were trained to hit a target with their first arrow. At first, they had laughed at Nathan's clumsiness, but now he could hit a running rabbit or squirrel with an arrow half of the times he shot.

He learned to move through the forest without making a sound. He left scarcely any trail to be followed. Being with the Indians sharpened those skills he had learned from Pa. His life depended on his abilities. Indians had no use for anyone who could not be useful to them or be respected by them. Nathan learned as quickly as he could. He still wanted to escape and return to Pa, but he thought that if they didn't escape, life wouldn't be so bad. He enjoyed hunting with the men and learning how to track the animals they needed. Like Pa, they only killed those they could use for food. Even the skins became clothing. Nothing was wasted.

Much of the smaller game they brought back to camp had been caught and skinned by Nathan. He was usually a bloody mess after skinning the animals. He didn't bother to wash afterward. No one cared whether he bathed or not. He could easily live with that.

Nathan knew that girls grow up quickly in the wilderness. Before long, Sarah would be considered by the Indians old enough to become a wife. He knew that they must get away before that happened or it never would. He had learned that the festival for choosing of the brides was to be soon. To prepare for the feasting of the occasion, all of the braves—and those they trusted—would bring in much meat. They would hunt daily. It was a good excuse for Nathan to make many arrows. He hoped that he would have some left for when he could manage the escape. They would get away or they would die. Nathan would make sure that no matter what happened he would save one arrow to make sure that Sarah was not captured again. Failing to escape would not be pleasant, especially for a girl. Indians had ways of showing their displeasure in ways that were too terrifying for Nathan to think about. One way or the other, he would save his sister.

CHAPTER THIRTEEN

A Good Hunt

Sarah's arms were piled high with wood. She didn't know how much wood she had carried that day. It seemed like a whole forest. With a clatter, she let the last logs fall on the ground. The woman who was stirring the meat in a big kettle dropped her paddle and yelled at Sarah.

"I wouldn't even care if she hit me," thought Sarah. "I'm just too tired to care."

She crept around to the back of the bark-covered quonset in which she slept and, feeling grateful, sat down on the hard ground. When she had rested for a while, she thought about their captivity. Several other captives were in the camp when she and Nathan had arrived. Three more were brought in yesterday. None of them had been hurt by the Indians.

It wasn't as bad in the village as she had feared. Most of the women were very kind to each other and to the children. All of the children seemed warm and loving to Sarah. She had as much to eat as anyone; in fact, she had more to eat now than she did at home. The Shawnees were good hunters and brought back plenty of game for the women to clean and cook. That meant plenty of skins that Sarah had to help cure. She didn't like having to scrape the hairs off the hides that were stretched on willow racks. She used a sharp stone as a scraper. Her hands were becoming calloused from the rock pressing in the same places on her palms.

Grinding the corn to make meal was something that she liked to do. She could sit by the big, hollowed-out rock and rub the dry kernels with a smaller stone until they looked like gold dust in the sun. The rhythm of the movement pleased her, and the sun felt good on her back. The corn smelled so clean and good—it was about the only thing in the village that did.

Never would she get used to the other smells. She even went out of her way to avoid the rocks where the fish were dried. She hated having to go into the quonset, where the odor of bear grease and unwashed bodies seemed so much stronger than in the open air. Sarah tried to keep herself as clean as she could. She was beginning to look like an Indian, but she was not going to smell like one if she could help it.

Being out in the sun so much had tanned her skin and turned her hair a coppery gold color. The only thing that distinguished her from the Indian girls was her blond hair and blue eyes. She wore her hair in a braid that hung down her back. The end of the braid was tied with a piece of rawhide thong. It was like the rawhide that the Indian had used to tie her wrists. She would always have scars on her wrists where the leather strap cut into her flesh.

The Indians did not mistreat her. They worked her hard enough, but Sarah didn't mind that too much. She was used to working hard. Gramma had always kept her busy. "The devil finds work for empty hands," Gramma would say and set Sarah on another task as soon as she had finished what she was doing.

The girl fought off a feeling of homesickness when she thought about Gramma. At least Nathan was in the same village with her, though she didn't see him often. They had tried to get alone and make a plan to escape, but so far they hadn't come up with one they thought would work.

Today, she hadn't seen Nathan at all. He had been taken along with the hunting party that had gone out soon as it was light. Of course, he wasn't trusted with a rifle. There were only two or three rifles in the village, and they were property of the biggest chiefs. One of those was the old muzzle-loader that belonged to Nathan when he was captured.

Nathan was strong and wiry for an almost thirteen year old. His job was to carry back the game that was killed. "Nathan sure would be a mess when he got back and stinkin' with the smell of animals he had carried," Sarah thought. "He'd smell as bad as the others."

For once she was glad that he slept in another shelter. She was thankful that she wouldn't have to smell him, too. Tonight she'd put the skins she slept on just as close to the opening of the quonset as she dared. The smells didn't seem to bother the Indian women, but they made Sarah's stomach heave.

The Indian women were excited about something. The women chattered constantly and were impatient with her slowness more than they had been when she first arrived. Sarah hadn't been a captive long enough to understand the strange, guttural language that they used. She hoped she wouldn't be in the village long enough to learn it, either. Though she did wish that she understood enough to know what was causing the whole camp to be in an uproar.

She'd better get back to the campfire before she was missed. The women left her pretty much alone, but if she were gone too long, they'd come looking for her. She'd kept this quiet place in the forest to herself and didn't want to be found here. It was the only place in the camp that she thought of as especially hers. Here, she felt like Sarah again instead of just a slave to an Indian woman.

She went for another armload of wood to carry to the fire. As she straightened up from dropping wood, she noticed that the hunting party was coming back. Sarah hurried over to join the women. She would have to help work on the meat. Loudly, the women grunted about the fine hunt, pleased with what the men laid before them.

Sarah took a step back as a young buck was placed at her feet. Startled, she looked up, and her eyes met those of the Indian who had captured her. What did he want, she wondered?

"Big feast," he said. "Many braves come. Pick wives."

There weren't many unmarried women in the village. There were several girls her age and a little older. She knew that the Indian girls were married young and taken to the quonset of the brave's family to care for her man's needs. Two young wives lived in the same shelter that Sarah did.

She looked at the buck lying before her. The Indian's feet were almost touching it. Puzzled, she looked at him again.

He grinned down at her. Waves of fear washed through her body. Terrified, she turned and ran.

CHAPTER FOURTEEN

A Plan is Made

Luke and Sam'l had been lying on the bluff above the Indian settlement since long before dawn. They were carefully hidden from the view of anyone looking up. For many weeks, they had watched the activity below and studied the habits of the Indians. Luke was impatient with the delay, but he knew that before they could act to free Sarah and Nathan it would be wise to know as much as possible. He was satisfied that the children were unharmed. Many times during the day, he would see Sarah moving about the camp. It seemed to Luke that she was being treated better than he had expected. She was worked hard, but not harder than she could bear.

Until today, the rescue party had seen Nathan only in the morning when he left with the hunting parties and again when they returned with the meat they had killed. No hunters went out today. They could see Nathan helping to burn out a log that was to become a dugout canoe. They had seen several other children who were not Indian in the village. Luke wondered what other families had been raided and how many had been taken to other places.

He noticed that Sarah didn't appear to be watched too closely by the women. They had all seemed to be too busy to pay much attention to what she was doing. Several times she had gone alone to the river for water.

Luke stopped chewing on a piece of jerky and watched as several braves he had not seen before came around the bend of the river. They were not painted. They had come in peace. The canoes they paddled were made of birch bark, not the hollowed out, shaped logs that were used by the Indians of the village. They must have come from farther north where birch canoes were more common. There was excitement in the camp over their coming. These braves must have been expected.

Slowly, Sam'l turned his head to look at Luke. There was a question in his eyes. Luke arched his eyebrows to show that he, too, was puzzled about the happenings. Something was in the air. There was no doubt about that, what with the bringing in of more meat than was needed and the bustle of the women. Might be a ceremony of some sort. They'd have to be patient until they knew what was happening.

"Wonder if Luke has made a plan yet? I'd rather walk a week without stoppin' than spy on some Redskins," Sam'l thought. Even though Sam'l was much younger than Luke, he was cramped from lying still so long. He would be glad when they could take some kind of action. He knew that what they were doing was the best thing, but that didn't mean he had to like it.

Luke had studied the way the bluff ran. With care, he could crawl down behind some bushes and reach the river. It was risky, but it was the only way he could think of to let Sarah know he was there. If he failed, Sam'l could go back for help. He'd watch for his chance. He signaled Sam'l what he planned to do. Now, he must force himself to wait for the best time to start. The warm sun was directly overhead when Luke saw that a huge fire was being built in front of the council house. Women were carrying great chunks of meat and putting them on spits. Everyone in the village seemed to be busy, and the sound of the activity reached the watchers on the bluff. It was time to move. Carefully, Luke wormed his way on his stomach to a clump of bushes near the water. He wanted to get closer to where Sarah usually went, but there was nothing large enough to hide him. He'd just have to wait here and hope to get her attention. He hoped that it would be Sarah who was sent for water. He watched as best he could without showing himself.

It seemed to him that it was hours before he heard someone coming. With great care, he raised himself to see who it was. His heart seemed to stop. It was Sarah, and she was alone. He wanted to jump out, grab her and run, but he knew that would be foolish. He must get her attention. He picked up a pebble that lay on the ground by his knee and lightly tossed it toward Sarah. Startled, she looked up and started to turn. "Don't look around! Keep on doin' what you're doin'! Don't turn!" he whispered to her as softly as he could. "Don't talk! Listen!"

She stood as though frozen. She couldn't believe her ears. Pa! It was Pa! How did he get here? How did he find her? Tears rolled down her cheeks.

"Come closer, but stay at the river. Slowly now. Act natural."

As though in a trance, she obeyed. She didn't believe that she wasn't dreaming.

"Sarah, find Nathan. Tell him when the feast is goin' strong he's to slip away to the river. He should go round through the woods to the dugouts and lay down inside the closest one to this bush. You count—slow—to a hundred when you see him leave. Then come down, like you been doin', to get water. Get in the dugout with Nathan. Remember, don't let anybody hear you talk to him. If you understand, take some water in your hands, like you was washin' your face."

Slowly, she bent over. She put both hands in the cool water and splashed it on her face. It was real! She wasn't dreaming! She washed her face again to be sure.

"Now go back up. Be careful to act like always, or you'll give yourself away." He wanted to turn and watch her go, but he didn't dare. He'd chanced too much already. Everything depended on Sarah. He prayed that she could carry it off. He dreaded the thought of what would happen if she didn't.

CHAPTER FIFTEEN

Celebration

Everyone in the village was gathered around the huge fire. It would be a great feast. The women chattered constantly as they stirred the stew and turned the spits. The young unmarried braves were still in the council house with the chiefs. The other men sat quietly and waited for them to come out. Many brave and tried warriors were in the village. They had been arriving throughout the afternoon. Most of them had come by way of the river. Their canoes were clustered closely together at the water's edge. Little Bird stood in the door of the quonset. They were ready to begin. They had much to celebrate tonight: the successful hunt, the many slaves taken in the raids, and the choosing of the brides. It was the choosing of the brides that had Sarah very worried.

A silence fell upon the Indians as the chief, Brave Wolf, stepped to the door of the quonset. Many strings of wampum hung around his neck. He was a great warrior who had counted much coup. Respectfully, they waited for his signal to begin the ceremony. With dignity, he raised his arm and looked over the people before him. It was good. He began to speak. He called upon the Great Spirit to see how strong the warriors were and what great hunters they were, also. He told of the many deer that had been killed. He named Red Arrow as the man who killed more deer than any other hunter. He told of the raids and named each man who had brought in a captive. He spoke for many minutes on what had been done. Finally, he named the warriors who could take a wife that night. As he named them, he told of each man's achievements. Each in turn, the brave of whom he spoke stood forward. The last was Running Deer, who had captured Sarah.

On the edge of the crowd, Sarah again felt fear when she saw him standing at the council house. She knew that she didn't dare run. That would call attention to her. She forced herself to stand unmoving through the speeches of the other chiefs. It seemed to her that hours went by before they stopped.

Each chief talked about the raids, the captives, the hunting. They said much the same thing that Brave Wolf had said. The Indians listened respectfully, as though they had never heard it before. They grunted agreement at each feat that was mentioned. It was the right of each man to be heard, they believed, and so the speeches went on until the last chief had spoken.

Again, Brave Wolf stood and raised his arm. "Let the feast begin," he called in a loud voice. As he dropped his arm, whoops and yells filled the air.

Sarah thought her head would split with the noise. The feasting and dancing began. Sarah was kept so busy helping the women serve the men that for a while she almost forgot where she was. She had managed to see Nathan earlier and had signaled him that she must speak to him. It had been too risky then. There were many people around. Now she was worried that she would not be able to find him in this crowd. As a slave, he was not seated with the men, and she was constantly being called by one or another woman to do something. She wished she could see Nathan.

Little Bird sent Sarah to stir the stew at the cooking fire. She could hardly see for the smoke that was coming from under the kettle. Someone must have put green logs on the flames. She hoped Little Bird wouldn't blame her for it. Her eyes stung from the smoke.

"Sarah! Sarah!" the whisper came from the edge of the woods. "Come over here, I made the fire smoke so they wouldn't see us talking. Hurry! I can't be gone long."

Sarah dropped the stirring paddle and ran toward Nathan's voice. "Nathan, only listen, don't talk." Quickly, she told him what Pa had said for him to do.

"You be where I can see you, or I won't know you're gone," she finished.

"It'll be about an hour before I can get loose from what I've got to do. Start watchin' then. I'll try to be on this side of the big bonfire. Now get back to your stirrin'; that woman is comin' this way."

By the time Little Bird reached the stew kettle, Sarah was stirring like she'd never been gone. Angry, Little Bird grunted at Sarah and pushed her aside. She bent and, fussing at Sarah, pulled the green log from the fire. Sarah didn't care what Little Bird thought or did. Her heart was pounding. Pa was here. He'd save them from the Indians. They'd be free in just a little while. She scooped up some of the stew and began to eat. It was best to have food inside her before they left. No telling when they'd be able to eat again. She wished she could take some for Pa, but that would be too dangerous. She must be very careful. Lost in her thoughts, she didn't notice that someone had come between her and the fire. When she finished the last of the stew, she licked her fingers clean and wiped them on the weeds. She would like to have washed her hands, but she couldn't go to the river until Nathan left.

She better get back to the stew and stir a while. She stood up and realized that she was not alone. Looking up, she saw Running Deer grinning at her as though he knew a secret. She felt as though her heart would stop. She gasped, turned and ran as fast as she could to the circle of women.

CHAPTER SIXTEEN

Walk Slowly

Sarah stayed as close as she could to the women. Impatiently, she waited for Nathan to come to where she could see him. Time had never passed so slowly for her. She was more afraid now than ever of Running Deer and wanted to be as far away from him as she could get.

The Indians were dancing around the fire. As they danced, their excitement grew and the dance became more and more wild. Sarah prayed that Nathan would hurry. She couldn't bear to wait much longer.

She tried to look as busy as possible so that she wouldn't be sent on an errand somewhere where she couldn't watch for Nathan. She was also watching Running Deer so that she could stay away from the Indians. Pa would get her away from here. She wondered where Pa was. He was watching her, she knew. She stayed in the light of the fire so he could see her.

Where was Nathan? She knew that it was much longer than an hour since they had last met. Surely she couldn't have missed seeing him. What if he had already gone? What should she do? She couldn't bear to be in this village without him. Fear closed her throat at the thought of being left behind. "Stop it, Sarah!" she shook herself. "You know Pa wouldn't leave you. You're gettin' fretted. Something has held Nathan back a while. He'll make sure you see him. He wouldn't leave you any more than Pa would," she told herself. "Get busy and keep watchin'."

She started gathering up scraps of meat and bones to feed to the dogs that, for once, were tied. Usually, they were underfoot everywhere in the village, but tonight they were kept out of the way—another thing to be thankful for, she realized.

As she walked back toward the women, she saw Nathan. Their eyes met, and Sarah knew that soon she would start counting to a hundred. Her heart was beating so hard she was sure it could be heard.

Sarah watched Nathan work his way slowly through the Indians. How could he be so calm? It seemed ages until he reached the woods. She started, "One, two, three . . . ." She made herself take a breath between each number.

One-hundred! Time to go. She left the spit she had been tending and picked up the pails that were used to carry water. "Not so fast, Sarah, just act like you're going for water. Don't look around. Act natural, like Pa said." So she talked to herself all the way to the river. Never had it seemed so far away from the village. It was so hard not to run. Finally, she reached the dugout. "Nathan," she whispered as she crawled into it. A big hand closed over her mouth.

CHAPTER SEVENTEEN

A Walk in the Woods

"Shh! Shhh! Sarah, it's me, Pa. Nathan's safe with Sam'l. I'll tell you later. As quiet as you can, go to that bush where I first talked to you and wait for me," he breathed into her ear. He lifted her over the side of the dugout and pointed her in the right direction.

Luke stepped out of the canoe and, leaving Sarah's and Nathan's footprints in the damp soil at the river's edge, he began to clear away all traces of his being anywhere near the canoe. He had already put several heavy stones into it. Slowly, he pushed it into the water and set it adrift. The current would take it downstream. He hoped to throw the Indians off the trail. Carefully backing toward the bush, he erased the tracks he and Sarah had made.

Now he took her hand and led her toward the water. He was careful to leave no trail. Together they stepped into the river, and Luke took Sarah on his back. Then he waded out until he was waist deep. Carrying Sarah, he began walking upstream, against the pull of the current, as quickly as he could. He walked for a good way before he came closer to the shore, where the going was easier. Finally, he headed to the shore. The forest at that place was thick and would give good cover.

He set Sarah on her feet and started into the trees. The pace he set was fast, and Sarah found it hard to keep up, but it wasn't fast enough for her. She was fearful of a recapture. Pa stopped and let her catch her breath for a moment. Then they started off again, moving uphill. It was harder going than ever.

Just as Sarah was feeling as though she couldn't get another full breath, Pa stopped again. He signaled that she should lie down on the ground, and he put his hand over her mouth to tell her not to speak. "I'll be back," he whispered. "Don't move."

At last, she had rested enough to raise her head. There was a glow that looked as though it were below the place where she lay. She crawled closer and saw that she was lying on a ridge far over the Indian village.

"Why had they come here? Where was Pa?"

From behind, a faint smell of bear grease and smoke came to her. She was afraid to turn her head.

CHAPTER EIGHTEEN

Run from the Ridge

Without making a sound, Nathan crawled up next to Sarah. Slowly, she let out the breath she was holding. Of course he smelled of cooked meat and bear fat; she probably did, too—they'd been working around the cooking fire all day. She sure was skittish!

Pa came up on the other side of her. There was a big man with him. That must be Sam'l. Not one word was spoken as they watched the village.

The Indians were still dancing around the fire. Sarah realized that they had not yet been missed. By the looks of the woodpile by the cooking fire, she figured they'd been gone about an hour. The heap of logs had gone way down. She was supposed to keep the pile up. Little Bird would soon wonder why Sarah hadn't carried more wood and would start looking for her.

Just as she had predicted, Sarah soon saw that the women were going in and out of the quonsets. Next, they started looking in the dark places. The dance suddenly stopped, and the high voices of the Indians faintly rose from the clearing. They knew the children were gone. The braves began to search along the edge of the woods. Several of them went into the forest. They had found Nathan's trail. Another party headed for the river. It took them only seconds to discover that the dugout had been pushed into the water and to find the tracks of Sarah and Nathan leading to it.

The alarm was sounded. The group of braves that had tracked Nathan burst out of the woods near the river. The Indians wasted no time. It was all too clear to them that the children had stolen a canoe and escaped. Quickly, they pushed the other canoes into the water and began to paddle downstream. That was what Luke had been waiting to see. The Indians had taken the bait. Now was the time to move—before they discovered that they had been tricked. When they did find out, they'd be as mad as hornets, Luke thought. They were mad enough now losing their captives, and their being children would make the Indians even madder. We'd better get away fast and make sure we don't get caught. If they catch us, they'll show no mercy.

He reached over Sarah and touched Nathan's shoulder as a signal to move. Taking Sarah's hand again, he pulled her to her feet. He squeezed her hand once, though, to say everything would be all right. As quietly as they could move, they started off into the woods. They had to make as much distance as they could. The Indians couldn't read tracks in the dark.

Luke led the way, pulling Sarah behind him. Nathan followed, and Sam'l brought up the rear. They kept moving, except for a few short rest stops, until daybreak. Sarah was more tired than she had ever been. She felt like she'd been walking in her sleep half the time. At last they stopped in a sheltered place. It was where the water had washed out part of a hill and the dirt made a kind of overhang. Gratefully, Sarah sank to the ground. Nathan lay down beside her. For the second time since they'd been taken, he slept with his arm over her.

Sam'l backtracked a ways and made sure they hadn't left a trail. Luke sat guard over his son and daughter and hoped to get them back safely to the fort. He brushed a tear from his eye and muttered, "I'm tryin', Lizabeth, I'm tryin'."

Once in the fort, he would tell where the other captives were. It would be their responsibility to get the other captives back from the Indians. He wished he could have freed them, too. He would be lucky to get these two to safety. Bad as it was, the others would have to wait.

Luke and Sam'l took turns, one on guard while the other slept. The children had been asleep about four hours when they were awakened. They didn't take time to eat. They started chewing on strips of jerky as they kept up a steady pace. They would travel until Sarah could go no farther without rest.

They were making good time until Sarah stumbled over a root and fell. She was so tired that she hadn't seen it. She tried to get up, but the pain in her ankle set her back down.

"Pa, I can't walk!" she cried, tears leaving little paths behind as they rolled down her dirty cheeks.

Luke knelt and felt of the bones. "It ain't broke. Just a bad pull, but you won't get nowhere on that foot." He looked around and saw some plantain leaves, which he picked. He wrapped them around Sarah's ankle, which was beginning to swell.

"I'll have to carry you. We can't stop here. It's too open."

"Luke, there's a cave of sorts somewhere close to here. I hunted this way a couple of years ago. If I remember right, it should be over this way," Sam'l said. He started off to the left. The others followed. It didn't take him long to find the cave. Luke laid Sarah on the floor inside, where she quickly went to sleep again.

"Looks safe enough, Sam'l. Don't know as I could have carried her far. She's an armload, though she don't look it. We've been pushin' hard. Guess we all could use a rest. I'm goin' to fashion a litter to carry Sarah. We can make better time than wearin' ourselves down carryin' her in turns."

"I'll help you, Luke. Ain't no Indians close to us yet."

They went into the forest to cut two saplings to use for poles and to find wild grape vines with which to lace them together. It would make a bed of sorts, on which Sarah could lie to be carried. They would be gone just a few minutes. The children were both asleep and safe enough, they thought.

Shortly after they left, an Indian stepped from behind a tree and cautiously started toward the cave. He appeared to be alone. He stepped into the mouth of the cave.

Sarah had tossed and turned, troubled by her dreams. The pain in her sprained ankle woke her, and she opened her eyes.

"Running Deer!"

With one long step, he reached Sarah. He scooped her up into his arms and headed for the trees. She was so terrified she couldn't even scream.

CHAPTER NINETEEN

Try Again

"Stop! Put that girl down!" Luke and Sam'l stepped out from the trees in front of the Indian. Both of them were pointing their rifles at the Indian.

"How in tarnation did you think you'd steal her again?" Luke asked.

The Indian stood silent before them, his head bowed. How could the white man know how he felt? He had lost much respect when the girl escaped. He loved her and had planned to name her as his bride at the ceremony and take her into the lodge of his father. She was his prize. She should have been proud to be chosen by Running Deer, brave warrior of the Shawnee. He had watched her all through the feasting. She had worked well. He felt that she would make a good wife for him after she learned the ways of the women.

When she had disappeared, he continued searching for signs of her even after dark. He must get her back. He had shown her that he had singled her out. Now she had scorned him and shamed him by running away.

It didn't seem to matter what happened to him now. He was disgraced. He could not go back to the tribe.

"What'll we do with this varmint, Luke?"

Luke studied the problem for a few minutes. He made up his mind. "We'll take him with us to the fort, Sam'l. We can use him to get the other captives back. The Indians will be movin' now that the hunt is over. Probably head back across the river where they belong. He'll know where the village moved."

Sam'l kept his rifle pointed at Running Deer while Luke went for Nathan and the litter they had made to carry Sarah.

They lifted Sarah onto it. Luke picked up the front poles and motioned for Running Deer to take the back. Sam'l, never taking his gun off Running Deer's back, followed them. Nathan took the lead.

Nathan had learned much about tracking from the Indians while on the hunting parties. Luke had to direct him only a few times.

Before they had started, Sam'l had gone back over the Indian's route and made sure that he was alone. He wondered how Running Deer had known that Sarah and Nathan were not in the canoe that had been sent adrift downstream. They questioned him, but he remained mute. Sam'l and Luke knew there was no way to make an Indian talk if he didn't want to. They'd probably never find out.

As they hiked through the forest, Running Deer kept alert for a chance to escape. He knew that Sam'l would shoot him, but if he could get away, he would bide his time until the settlers thought they were safe. Then he would kidnap the girl again and return in glory to his people.

Right now, it looked like he'd have to be patient and do what these men wanted.

Running Deer knew how to be patient. It was a lesson he'd been taught early. For days, he had watched at the cabin until he saw that it was a good time to signal his men to raid. He'd waited at the camp seeing Sarah work with the women until he knew that she would be a good wife for him. Then he had decided to choose her. When the braves had followed the dugout and found it empty against the bank of the river, he had not given up. Carefully, he'd gone over the ground on both sides of the village until he'd found the place where Luke and Sarah had come out of the water. Then he followed their trail, backtracking when he'd lost it. He'd not slept nor eaten but pushed on until he had been captured. Now the Indian knew that the lessons of patience had been forgotten in his eagerness to save his honor. Running Deer shrugged. It was time to wait and watch again.

As they made their way through the forest, Sarah watched Running Deer. "What was there about him that frightens me so?" she wondered. She had no fear now, because Pa and Sam'l were there. Rubbing the scar on her wrist, she looked at him, curiously. He looked like any other Indian as far as she could tell. She was glad that he was carrying the foot of the litter. He smelled like any other Indian, too. However, there was something about him that bothered her. What could it be? His hair was black and tied in the Shawnee way. Dark eyes glittered from the copper color of his face. His body was lean and glistened with grease.

He shifted his hands to get a better grip on the poles he carried. Sarah was drawn to the movement to look at them. Her eyes widened in surprise as she saw his wrist. There were thong marks on it, too, just like hers. He, too, had once been a captive. But by whom?

CHAPTER TWENTY

The Indian Way

When they arrived at the clearing in front of the fort, a big cheer went up. They must look like a bedraggled band coming out of the woods, thought Sarah. Several men ran out to help. Two took the litter and carried Sarah the rest of the way to Martha's house. Some others bound Running Deer's hands and put a noose over his head, tightening it around his chest and dragging him into the fort. The women prepared a feast that evening, as everyone was relieved that Luke and Sam'l had rescued Sarah and Nathan.

After they had been at the fort for several weeks, Sarah's ankle finally healed and returned to normal. Pa had told the men about the captives and the Indian villages, and some of the men had gone to see if they could recover some or all of the other captives.

Since they had reached the fort, Running Deer had been locked in a cabin that was used for storage. There was no window in it. Someone always stood guard at the door. He had been questioned for days, but they got nothing from him. He lay on his pallet and refused to eat. He had lived as an Indian too long to even remember a time when he was taken. Being watched so closely showed him that there was no way he could escape.

Sarah often thought about him while her ankle was mending. When she was able to walk, she made up her mind to find out more about him. She no longer feared him; instead, she felt a curious sympathy for him. Both of them had been captured. If Pa hadn't saved her in time, she, too, might have become as much an Indian as Running Deer.

She had gone to the cabin where he was kept. She went to the door and called to him through the small opening that let air into the little room where he lay.

He took no more notice of her than he did of anyone else. "Running Deer," she called. "I want to talk to you. Come to the door."

"Running Deer," she tried again. "It's Sarah. I want to help you. Tell me who your parents are. I know you were captured. If we can find your folks, you can go back to them."

He lay as though he had turned to stone.

Slowly, Sarah turned away. She tried twice more, without any success, to get him to respond.

Luke tried to explain to her that the young man had lived with the Indians for so long that he believed himself to be one. This often happened when a boy is captured so young. It could have happened to Nathan.

Trapped in a shed, Running Deer turned his face to the wall. What did the girl know about freedom? He saw no way out of his shame. He would not live as a caged animal. He made up his mind he would escape or die. It was the Indian way.

CHAPTER TWENTY-ONE

Decision

"Pa, when are we goin' home?" Nathan asked. "It's high time we got the corn in the ground. I was talkin' to Matthew the other day, and he said he had some extra corn seed he could let us have."

Luke had been thinking, too. The confinement of the fort was beginning to wear on him. There were too many people around. Particularly widow Schmidt, a former teacher, and her endless chatter. She gave him the willies. He also knew that her first name was Jane and she was a beautiful and lonely lady. She had light red hair and blue eyes. She had told him that she had come from Ireland but had married an elderly German man, who had died over a year ago. Sometimes he wished that he had the patience to know her better, as he knew that he didn't want to live alone for the rest of his life. But he had been so hurt by Lizabeth's death that he was afraid to risk loving another woman again. He was used to the quiet of the woods and longed to return.

Living in the cabin with James and his family troubled Luke. They were already crowded before they added three more people. Martha, James's wife, was a good woman. She was always bustling about, helping everyone, but her tongue was never still. Her constant chatter often drove Luke out of the house.

Lizabeth had been easy about her work. She never seemed to be in a hurry. Everything she had to do was done when it should be, but without the flutter that Martha had about her. His wife had never felt the need to talk about every little thing that went on. When she had something to say she said it, and that was only after she thought it out before she spoke.

Sarah was enamored with Martha. Martha helped Sarah with her reading and learning to speak the English language like a lady. Luke could understand the attraction, as Martha was the first woman Sarah could talk to since their capture.

Gramma's death and the death of Ben and Mary were hard for Sarah and Nathan. Luke didn't think Sarah would stop crying after he told her. He had saved that bad news until they got to the fort. Nathan was stoic. He had suspected as much anyway.

Luke missed Gramma and the small children. He didn't want to go home and see their graves, nor did he want to stay in the fort. The conflict was deep inside him. On the one hand, he would like to give up and go back to Pennsylvania. On the other, he had promised the children that they could rebuild the cabin and have a fresh start. For the first time in his life, he didn't know what to do.

Sarah decided for him. She knew it was time to go.

"Let's go home, Pa. There ain't nothin' in the fort for us. Ain't much left back home either, but you promised Ma when you built the stone chimney it would last a lifetime. Lets go see if you were right."

ABOUT THE AUTHORS

Ernest Matuschka, a Nebraskan, grew up in a small town, which afforded him the opportunity to hunt and fish as a youth.

Shortly after graduation from college, he entered the U.S. Air Force—during the Korean war—where he served as an intelligence officer.

Following his military service, he taught school in Colorado, in California and in Paris, France, where he was a guidance counselor, later moving to Germany, where he taught academic subjects and also served as Director of Guidance at the Mannheim American School. It was in Germany that he met his writing partner, Elizabeth Durbin. The Durbins and the Matuschkas had ten children between them, and they (and their families) became fast friends during the two years they were together.

The Matuschkas returned to California at the end of their German experience, and a few years later, Ernest applied for a leave of absence to complete work on his Ph.D. in clinical psychology. When he earned that degree, he and his family returned to Nebraska, where Ernest took a teaching position at the University of Nebraska at Kearney and opened a small private practice.

Ernest has written a number of professional articles for peer review psychology journals, authored two books on genealogy, and translated a book from German to English.

He retired from teaching and from practice in 1990. With their children grown and gone, the couple now lives fulltime in Chandler (Sun Lakes), Arizona.

Elizabeth Durbin is a retired teacher. She was born in Wisconsin and because her father was an army officer the family moved often, settling finally in Bowling Green, Kentucky, where Betty earned both bachelor's and master's degrees in education at Western Kentucky University. After teaching at the university for a year, Betty began a series of assignments at military bases, first at Fort Knox, Kentucky and then at Mannheim, Germany. Returning to the States, she taught in California and finally in Kentucky for the last 24 years of her career. Her specialties were Art and English.

A mother of six, Betty first told stories then committed them to writing so her children could read them. She lives full-time in Bowling Green but spends summers at a cabin at Barren River Lake, Kentucky, a home she built from the ground up.

Cole Matuschka, who produced the interior text illustrations for this book, is a freelance artist in Sellersburg, Indiana, where he lives with his parents and one brother. He intends to follow his passion for art by pursuing a degree at nearby Indiana University Southeast.

CPSIA information can be obtained
at www.ICGtesting.com
Printed in the USA
FFHW02n1855150918
48364325-52217FF